Wendel's Workshop

About the author:

Chris Riddell has written and illustrated over one hundred books for children and adults. He's won many book awards along the way too! Chris invents his characters in a shed at the bottom of his garden — and it is much tidier than Wendel's workshop.

For My Father

First published 2007 by Macmillan Children's Books
This edition published 2013 by Macmillan Children's Books
a division of Macmillan Publishers Limited
20 New Wharf Road, London N1 9RR
Basingstoke and Oxford
Associated companies throughout the world
www.panmacmillan.com

ISBN: 978-1-4472-8216-7

Text and illustrations copyright © Chris Riddell 2007
Moral rights asserted

2 4 6 8 9 7 5 3 1

A CIP catalogue record for this book is
available from the British Library.

Printed in China

Wendel's Workshop

Chris Riddell

MACMILLAN CHILDREN'S BOOKS

Wendel was
an inventor.

Sometimes his inventions
worked perfectly,
and sometimes
they didn't.

When they didn't,
Wendel just threw
them away and
started again.

Wendel invented all day and into the night.
Sometimes he was so busy inventing he forgot
to go to bed. And he never had time to tidy up.

Wendel's workshop became
untidier . . .   and untidier . . .   and UNTIDIER.

"I need some help," said Wendel to himself.

So Wendel invented a robot.

"I'll call you Clunk," said Wendel.
Clunk set to work tidying Wendel's workshop.

He made the
bed . . .

folded the
clothes . . .

and mopped
the floor.

"Oh dear," said Wendel.

Clunk tried harder.

He put the teacups in
the sock drawer . . .

and filled the
laundry basket
with umbrellas.

"This isn't working," said Wendel.

So he threw Clunk down the rubbish chute . . .

CLUNK!

. . . and out onto the scrapheap.

Inside the workshop,
Wendel was inventing
a new robot.

He worked all night . . .

and into the morning.

At last it was finished.

"I'll call you the Wendelbot," said Wendel.
"Tidy!" said the Wendelbot, its red eyes glowing.
"Tidy!" And it set to work.

The Wendelbot worked perfectly.
Wendel was very pleased.

But the Wendelbot didn't stop. Its red eyes glowed as it unmade the bed into a neat bundle, and crushed the teacups to a tidy pile of powder.

"Tidy!" the Wendelbot said as it shredded the umbrellas, and flattened the laundry basket. "Tidy!" Soon everything was neat and tidy.

All except one thing . . .

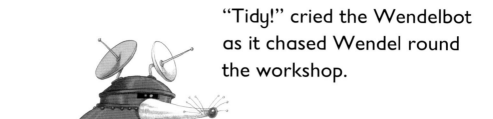

"Tidy!" cried the Wendelbot
as it chased Wendel round
the workshop.

"He-e-e-e-lp!" squeaked
Wendel as he shot
down the rubbish
chute . . .

. . . and out onto the scrapheap. Then, from quite close by, Wendel heard a clunk.

CLUNK!

"I'm SO pleased to see you!" said Wendel.

From inside the workshop, the noise of the Wendelbot's hammering and bashing grew louder and louder.

"We need some help," said Wendel,
"but all we've got is rubbish!"
Clunk reached down and handed
Wendel an interesting
piece of scrap.

Wendel smiled. And then he began to invent.

All day and into the night,
Wendel and Clunk were
hard at work.

As the sun rose, the hammering and bashing from Wendel's workshop stopped. "Workshop tidy!" said the Wendelbot. It turned its glowing red eyes towards the window. "NOW, TIDY WORLD!"

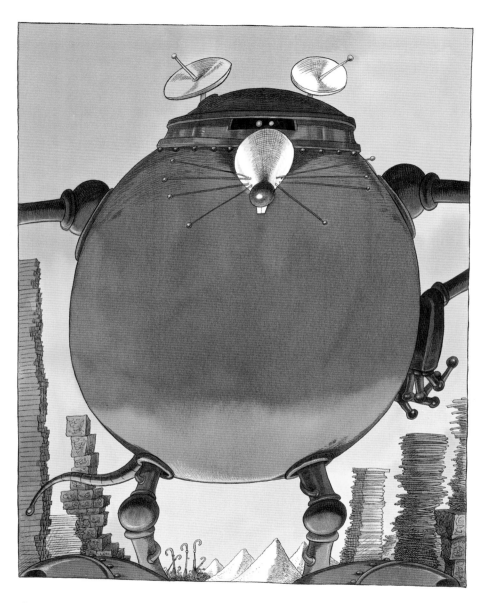

The Wendelbot strode across the workshop and threw open the door.

"Good morning," said Wendel.

The Wendelbot's eyes glowed red. "Tidy!" it said.
"Untidy! Untidy!" Wendel and his robot helpers
shouted as they ran inside.

"TIDY!" cried the Wendelbot, lumbering after them. But the robots were too quick for it.

The Wendelbot's eyes glowed brighter and brighter as Wendel's workshop grew untidier and untidier.

"Ti-i-ide . . .   Ti-i-i . . . d-eeeeee! TI-I-I . . . D-E-E-E!"

When the dust had settled, Wendel sighed. "Now we'll have to tidy up again," he said. "But not too much this time."

All the robots helped . . .

in their different ways.

Not everything
worked perfectly . . .

but Wendel didn't mind.
He just smiled, patched
this, mended that, and
made adjustments
here and there.

But there was one thing he didn't do . . .

Wendel NEVER threw anything on the scrapheap again.